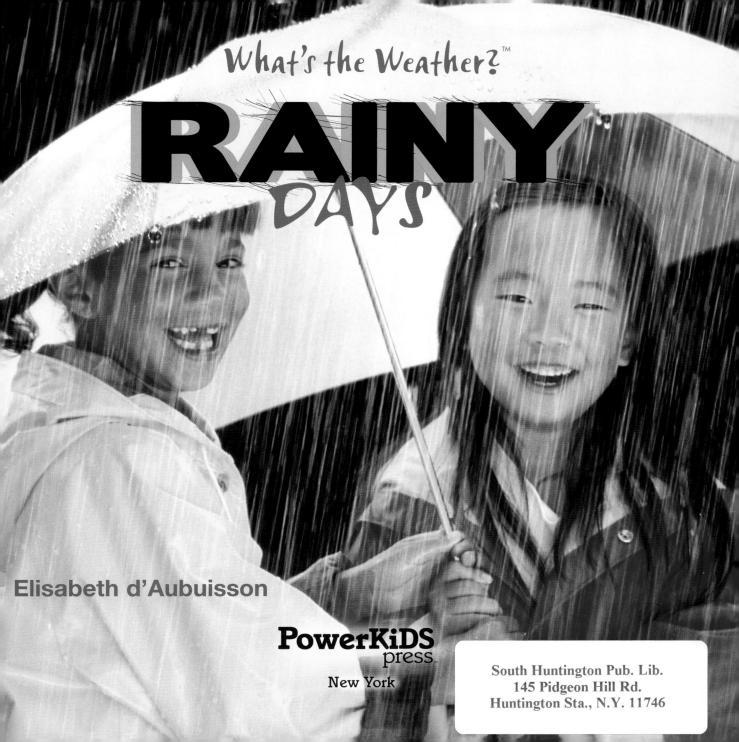

What's the Weather?™

RAINY
DAYS

Elisabeth d'Aubuisson

PowerKiDS press
New York

South Huntington Pub. Lib.
145 Pidgeon Hill Rd.
Huntington Sta., N.Y. 11746

551.577
D'Aubuisson

Published in 2007 by The Rosen Publishing Group, Inc.
29 East 21st Street, New York, NY 10010

Copyright © 2007 by The Rosen Publishing Group, Inc.

All rights reserved. No part of this book may be reproduced in any form without permission in writing from the publisher, except by a reviewer.

First Edition

Editor: Amelie von Zumbusch
Book Design: Julio Gil
Photo Researcher: Sam Cha

Photo Credits: Cover, p. 1 © Steve Satushek/Getty Images; pp. 5, 13 Shutterstock.com; p. 7 by Greg Tucker; pp. 9, 15, 21 © Getty Images; pp. 11, 17 © Artville; p. 19 © Digital Stock.

Library of Congress Cataloging-in-Publication Data

D'Aubuisson, Elisabeth.
   Rainy days / Elisabeth D'Aubuisson. — 1st ed.
       p. cm. — (What's the weather?)
   Includes index.
   ISBN-13: 978-1-4042-3682-0 (library binding)
   ISBN-10: 1-4042-3682-1 (library binding)
   1. Rain and rainfall—Juvenile literature. 2. Meteorology—Juvenile literature. I. Title.
   QC924.7.D375 2007
   551.57'7—dc22

                                              2006027267

Manufactured in the United States of America

Contents

What Is Rain?

Have you ever noticed that it rains only when there are clouds? This is because rain comes from clouds. Clouds are made of drops of water or ice. Clouds form when **water vapor** in the air becomes so cold it turns into water. Some of the drops of water group together to make larger drops of water. Other drops of water become so cold that they turn to ice. When the water drops or ice bits become heavy enough, they fall from the sky as rain or snow.

Raindrops often look like lines of water as they fall from the sky.

The Water Cycle

The water vapor that makes clouds forms when the **liquid** water in lakes, oceans, rivers, puddles, and streams **evaporates**. Water evaporates when the Sun shines on it and warms it up. You cannot see it, but evaporation takes place all the time.

A drop of water that was in the ocean today could become part of a cloud tomorrow. The next day that same drop of water could fall on you as a raindrop. The way that water moves through these different states is called the water **cycle**.

Rain Falls

Water Vapor
Forms Clouds

Water
Evaporates

Water Flows
Into Rivers

Rivers Join the Ocean

This picture shows how water moves through the water cycle.

Rain Gear

Though it is fun to walk in the rain, always wear rain gear to keep yourself warm and dry. One kind of rain gear is a raincoat. Raincoats are made from special cloth that repels, or keeps out, the rain. In heavy rainstorms people also wear hats or pants made from this special cloth. It is also a good idea to wear rain boots, or galoshes, to keep your feet dry.

Many people use **umbrellas** to stay dry. People have used umbrellas for thousands of years. Early umbrellas guarded people from the sun, not the rain.

This girl and her mother are doing their best to stay dry on a rainy day in Honolulu, Hawaii.

Inside Fun

A rainy day is an excellent time to be inside. You can listen to the rain tapping on your roof and windows or curl up with a good book. Playing or listening to music is another good way to spend a rainy day.

Rainy days are great times to play games. You can pick a board game, like chess and checkers, or a computer game. There are lots of card games you could pick. If you get an adult to help you, you could even bake cookies or build a birdhouse!

These girls are spending a rainy day inside. They are playing a board game called mancala.

Outdoor Fun

There are plenty of things to do outside on a rainy day. Walking in the rain is a great way to see animals, such as ducks, that like rain.

You can also make a rain **gauge**. Take a clear jar with a flat bottom. Put it in a flat place that does not have a roof or tree right above it. When the rain stops, use a ruler to measure how much water is in your rain gauge. This will tell you how many inches (cm) of rain fell.

The rain gauges that are sold in stores often have inches (cm) marked on the outside.

Kinds of Rain

If you use a rain gauge often, you will notice that some days a lot of rain falls in just a few hours. Other days it keeps raining all day long, but you get only a little water.

This is because there are many kinds of rain. People have many words they use to describe different kinds of rain. A light rain is called a mist or a **drizzle**. A heavy rain is called a downpour. Some people say, "It's raining cats and dogs" when it rains very hard.

These people got caught in a downpour in London, England.

Thunderstorms

One striking kind of rainstorm is a **thunderstorm**. Along with rain thunderstorms have lightning. Lightning happens when rain clouds build up a lot of natural **electricity**. This makes a **bolt** of lightning cut across the sky. A lightning bolt makes a loud roar, called thunder. You see lightning bolts before you hear thunder, because light moves faster than sound does.

You can be badly hurt if lightning hits you. Try to stay inside during a thunderstorm. If you are outdoors, stay away from high hills and tall trees. Lightning often strikes the highest point.

Lightning strikes somewhere on Earth about 100 times each second.

Why We Need Rain

Though thunderstorms can be scary and rainstorms can keep you from playing outside, all life on Earth needs rain. Plants need water to grow. Animals and people need water to drink. In fact, kids should drink 6 to 8 cups (1–2 l) of water a day.

If too little rain falls, it will cause a **drought**. The soil dries out during a drought. Plants dry up and die. The animals that eat these plants cannot find food. The dried plants and dusty soil make it easier for forest fires to start, too.

Horses need rain. They drink water that once fell as rain.
They also eat grass that needs rain to grow.

Too Much Rain

Although people, plants, and animals all need rain, too much rain can cause problems. When it rains much of the rainwater goes into the ground. If it rains heavily, the ground gets wet and soft. When the soft, wet ground is part of a hill, a big chunk of earth can slide downhill. This is called a landslide. Landslides can cover houses and roads.

Too much water also causes floods. Floods happen when rivers and streams are so full they run over. A flood can cover streets, stores, and houses in several feet (m) of water.

The water was too deep for this boy to ride his bike during a flood in Cynthiana, Kentucky.

Rain in Our World

Rain causes problems, but we could not live without it. Rain supplies the water that crops need to grow. It keeps forests healthy and helps stop forest fires. People use rainwater for drinking, cleaning, and gardening.

It is important to keep the water that moves through the water cycle clean. If just one pond becomes **polluted**, the pollution can spread throughout the water cycle. However, if we all work to keep our water clean, the water cycle will continue to supply us with the rain we need for many years to come.

Glossary

bolt (BOLT) A stroke of lightning.

cycle (SY-kul) Actions that happen in the same order over and over.

drizzle (DRIH-zul) Rain in fine, misty drops.

drought (DROWT) A period of dryness that hurts crops.

electricity (ih-lek-TRIH-suh-tee) Power that produces light, heat, or movement.

evaporates (ih-VA-puh-rayts) Changes from a liquid to a gas.

gauge (GAYJ) A thing that tells facts about something.

liquid (LIH-kwed) Matter that flows.

polluted (puh-LOO-ted) Full of waste that hurts Earth's air, land, or water.

thunderstorm (THUN-dur-storm) A storm with flashes of lightning and loud sounds called thunder.

umbrellas (um-BREH-luz) Circles of cloth on folding sticks.

water vapor (WAH-ter VAY-pur) The gaseous state of water.

Index

Web Sites

Due to the changing nature of Internet links, PowerKids Press has developed an online list of Web sites related to this book. This site is updated regularly. Please use this link to access the list:

www.powerkidslinks.com/wtw/rainy/

SEP 2 6 2007

21²⁵